Sleeping Beauty

Illustrated by Tika and Tata

Miles Kelly

Once upon a time a beautiful baby girl was born to a king and queen. They had wanted a child for a long time, so they were very happy.

The proud king soon began
organizing a birthday celebration
for the little princess.

The king and queen invited all
their friends and family.

They also asked the fairies
to come, all apart from one,
who was known for being mean.

On the big day, guests arrived, bringing lots of lovely gifts.

"Congratulations your highnesses!"

The fairies lined up to give the
baby princess their gifts.

One by one they came forward, giving
gifts of kindness, courage and cleverness.

The last fairy was just about to give her gift, when there was a loud noise in the courtyard.

Crash!

Just then, the mean fairy, who had not been invited, burst in angrily and said,

"When the princess is sixteen she shall touch a spindle and die."

The king and queen gasped in shock. But then the last fairy stepped forward. "Wait!" she said.

"I can soften the curse a little," the fairy said. "If the princess touches a spindle, she will not die."

"Instead, she will fall asleep for one hundred years. Only a prince shall be able to wake her with a single kiss."

The king gave an order
for all the spindles in
the land to be destroyed.

The princess grew up to be a kind, thoughtful young lady.

One day, while exploring the castle, she came across a door that she hadn't seen before.

She opened it and found steps leading up to a mysterious room.

The princess walked up the steps into the room. There she saw a strange woman, busy at a strange wheel with some thread.

"Hello, what are you doing?" asked the princess.

"I'm spinning, my dear," said the woman. The princess walked closer, and as she came to the spindle she reached out to touch it.

Whrrrrr whrrrrr!

"Ouch!" The princess cried out as her finger touched the spindle. The wicked fairy, for it was she, vanished, and the princess fell into a deep sleep.

At that moment the king and queen fell asleep on their thrones. The horses slept in their stables and the servants slipped into a slumber.

Days, weeks, and then months
went past, and a large hedge of
thorns grew around the palace. Every
year it became thicker, until the
palace was completely hidden

One hundred years later, a prince rode by. He saw the tips of a tower above the thorns. As he neared, the thorns parted, allowing him through.

The prince eventually arrived at the palace and saw that everyone was sleeping.

He wondered why everything and everyone had been frozen in time.

He came to the room where the princess was sleeping. She was so beautiful that he stooped to kiss her. Then she opened her eyes and smiled.

It was love at first sight.

Everyone else in the castle also awoke. At last the princess was reunited with her mother and father.

The evil fairy's spell had been broken!

Sleeping Beauty and the prince were married, and lived happily ever after!

"Hip hip hooray!"